4·2

Jeremy Strong once worked in a bakery, putting the jam into three thousand doughnuts every night. Now he puts the jam in stories instead, which he finds much more exciting. At the age of three, he fell out of a first-floor bedroom window and landed on his head. His mother says that this damaged him for the rest of his life and refuses to take any responsibility. He loves writing stories because he says it is 'the only time you alone have complete control and can make anything happen'. His ambition is to make you laugh (or at least snuffle). Jeremy Strong lives in Kent with his wife, Susan, a cat or two, and something in the attic that makes scratching noises at night, but he hasn't found out what it is yet.

Jeremy Strong

VIKING
at School

PUFFIN BOOKS

PUFFIN BOOKS

Published by the Penguin Group
Penguin Books Ltd, 80 Strand, London WC2R 0RL, England
Penguin Putnam Inc., 375 Hudson Street, New York, New York 10014, USA
Penguin Books Australia Ltd, 250 Camberwell Road, Camberwell, Victoria 3124, Australia
Penguin Books Canada Ltd, 10 Alcorn Avenue, Toronto, Ontario, Canada M4V 3B2
Penguin Books India (P) Ltd, 11 Community Centre, Panchsheel Park, New Delhi – 110 017, India
Penguin Books (NZ) Ltd, Cnr Rosedale and Airborne Roads, Albany, Auckland, New Zealand
Penguin Books (South Africa) (Pty) Ltd, 24 Sturdee Avenue, Rosebank 2196, South Africa

Penguin Books Ltd, Registered Offices: 80 Strand, London WC2R 0RL, England

www.penguin.com

First published by A & C Black Publishers Ltd 1997
Published in Puffin Books 2001
1

Text copyright © Jeremy Strong 1999
All rights reserved

The moral right of the author has been asserted

Set in Monotype Baskerville

Typeset by Rowland Phototypesetting Ltd, Bury St Edmunds, Suffolk
Made and printed in England by Clays Ltd, St Ives plc

British Library Cataloguing in Publication Data
A CIP catalogue record for this book is available from the British Library

ISBN 0–141–31485–0

1 The Biggest Wrestling Match in the World

Mrs Tibblethwaite flew through the air, looking rather like an overstuffed rag-doll, and landed with an immense thud on the floor. She picked herself up and sighed groggily. It was strange being part of a top wrestling team. She stood and watched as a very large and scruffy Viking warrior zoomed over her head and crashed into the front row of the audience. Mrs Tibblethwaite sighed again. It was even stranger being married to a real Viking.

She climbed out of the ring and tried to pull Sigurd from the laps of three startled, elderly ladies, but they clung on to him and threatened Mrs Tibblethwaite with their bulging handbags.

'We're going to keep him!' screeched the lady with huge, horn-rimmed glasses.

'You can't keep him,' explained Mrs Tibblethwaite. 'We are in the middle of a wrestling match, and besides, he's my husband.'

'Well you can't have him,' insisted the lady

with thick brown stockings, locking both her arms round Sigurd's hairy head. 'He belongs to us. We're his fan club.'

This was too much for Sigurd. The prospect of being carried off by three old age pensioners was a real blow to his pride. A Viking being kidnapped by women! It was unheard of! He was supposed to capture them! Sigurd leapt to his feet and scowled at the three old ladies. He'd show them!

'I kidnap you!' he cried. 'I take you home. Now I have three sleeves.'

The ladies looked at Sigurd, glanced at each other and shook their heads with bewilderment. 'You've only got two arms,' observed the horn-rimmed glasses, 'so how come you've got three sleeves?' But before they could say anything more Sigurd began to pluck them from their seats.

'You my sleeves!' he cried, tossing brown-stockings over his shoulder. 'You do anything I say!'

Mrs Tibblethwaite shook her head. 'I think you mean "slave", Sigurd, not "sleeve". Anyway, they can't be your slaves. That sort of thing isn't allowed any more.'

'We don't mind!' cried the three old ladies,

hanging halfway down Sigurd's back. 'We love Siggy – he's our hero!'

Mrs Tibblethwaite shut her eyes and sat down on the edge of the wrestling ring. This was always happening. Whenever they appeared as one of the country's top tag-wrestling teams half the old women in the audience fainted and swooned. They threw their hankies at Sigurd, and their pension books. And they always tried to sneak off with him.

Suddenly, Mrs Tibblethwaite was brought back to life by a loud and angry voice from above her head. 'Oi! Are you two fighting us or not?' shouted Bone-Cruncher Boggis, leaning over the ropes.

He had a shiny, bald head and he was wearing a black, spangly leotard with 'MAD AND BAD' written across the front in silver letters. He reached down with a long, hairy arm and grabbed Mrs Tibblethwaite by one ear.

'Ow!'

Sigurd dropped the three ladies at once and rushed across to help his wife. 'You leave my Tibby!' he cried. 'You nasty big belly!'

'Who are you calling a big belly?' demanded Monster Mash, Bone-Cruncher's partner.

'He means bully,' squawked Mrs
Tibblethwaite. 'He's calling you a big bully. Ow!'

Sigurd was not going to put up with any
more of this. He leapt into the ring and seized
Bone-Cruncher by one leg, dragging him across
the floor. Monster Mash threw himself on top of
Sigurd and all four of them rolled round and
round the ring, making various squashed and
squidged noises such as 'Oof!' and 'Urrrff!' Then
Monster Mash jumped on top of Sigurd, and
struck a triumphant pose. The breath came out of
Sigurd's flattened chest like the air rushing from a
whoopee cushion . . .

'Ssppllllrrrrrrrrrr!'

The three pensioners watched in dismay.
Their hero was about to be beaten! In
desperation, they clambered into the ring and
started attacking Monster Mash and Bone-
Cruncher with their handbags. 'Take that!'

'Leave Siggy alone!'

'Bullies!'

The poor referee tried to intervene, but he
was quickly caught in the crossfire of several
whirling handbags and sank to the floor
unconscious. Other members of the audience
hurried from their seats to join in the battle. Some

of them were fans of Monster Mash and Bone-Cruncher and it was not long before the entire wrestling ring was filled with noisy, struggling bodies. After a few minutes, the fight spilled out beyond the ropes, on to the floor, up the aisles and amongst the audience.

Then the police arrived – all four of them. It wasn't enough of course and they sent for reinforcements. Thirty more policemen hurried to the scene. But that wasn't enough either. By now, the entire audience was at each other's throats. Even more reinforcements were sent for and eventually the fire brigade arrived and hosed everyone down. That stopped the fighting, but it didn't stop the quarrelling.

'Who started it?' demanded Inspector Hole, tipping a litre of water out of his hat.

'He did!'

'No – she did!'

'It was the Viking!'

Fingers pointed in every direction, but mostly they pointed at Sigurd. He crawled out from beneath a squelchy pile of bodies, looking rather bedraggled. Inspector Hole sized him up cautiously. Oh yes! Here was the culprit if ever there was one.

'Dressing up as a Viking eh?' he sniggered. 'That's a bit childish, isn't it?'

Mrs Tibblethwaite bristled. 'He's a real Viking,' she snapped.

'Oh yes? And how's that then?' the inspector smirked.

'Sigurd sailed to England in a Viking longship with a raiding party a thousand years ago. He got separated from the others, went through some kind of Time-mist and ended up in our time; now he's my husband.'

Inspector Hole wrinkled his nose. 'Sounds like you've been watching too many fantasy films,' he muttered. 'Right then, let's see – causing a disturbance – that's about five years in prison. Fighting in public, assault, starting a riot, damaging property – and didn't you say he was some kind of raider? That's definitely not allowed nowadays. Must be another forty years or so . . .'

'You can't send him to prison!' cried Mrs Tibblethwaite.

'Yes you can!' shouted the referee. 'He's a menace to society – they both are. If it hadn't been for them, this would never have happened. Look at my wrestling hall! It will cost thousands of pounds to repair all this.'

Inspector Hole fished around in his pockets for a pair of handcuffs. Sigurd looked most upset. 'I good boy,' he muttered.

'Yes he is,' agreed one of the pensioners. 'It wasn't his fault, officer. If you try and send him to prison we shall complain to the Police Authorities.' Sigurd grinned cheerfully at Inspector Hole.

'They my sleeves,' he explained somewhat confusingly.

Inspector Hole heaved a deep, deep sigh. It was obvious the crowd would make trouble if he tried to arrest the Viking and his wife. 'Okay everyone,' he grumbled. 'The fun's over. You'd better all go home before I decide to make a mass arrest.'

The referee was beside himself. 'Aren't you going to do anything?' he demanded. 'My hall is ruined.'

'Nothing I can do I'm afraid,' said the inspector, but the referee wasn't going to put up with this.

'Okay. If you won't do anything, I will.' He fixed Mrs Tibblethwaite and Sigurd with a stern eye. 'You two are banned,' he declared, 'and not just in my wrestling hall, but anywhere in the world. You'll never wrestle again. You're banned for life!' The ref turned and stalked back inside his sodden hall.

Inspector Hole grinned maliciously. 'Well, it looks like you two are out of a job,' he sniggered. 'Serves you right,' he added as he got into his car and drove off. The fire brigade packed away their hoses and drove off. Slowly, the crowd began to squelch back to their homes. Even the three old ladies shuffled away, quietly crying into their cardigans.

It took a little while for Sigurd to understand what had happened. 'No more bish-bash?' he asked. Mrs T. shook her head. 'No more squish-squash?'

'No,' said Mrs Tibblethwaite.

'No more leg-wrinkles and head-crinkles?'

'NO!' shouted Mrs Tibblethwaite impatiently.

'You cross,' he observed.

'Yes! I'm cross!'

'You very cross.'

'Yes! I'm very cross!' cried Mrs Tibblethwaite.

'You very, very, VERY cross!' said Sigurd.

'Oh for goodness' sake shut up!' yelled poor

Mrs Tibblethwaite, and she belted Sigurd so hard with her handbag that it stuck on one of his helmet horns.

As he struggled to pull it off, the clasp on the bag opened and half her belongings tinkled out through the hole.

Mrs Tibblethwaite wearily got down on her hands and knees and began to pick everything up. 'I wish you understood how serious this is, Siggy,' she told him. 'We shall never be able to wrestle again. We have no work, and that means we have no money. How are we going to live?'

Sigurd looked at his wife with a cheerful grin. 'Easy-peasy, Japanesey,' he said. 'We go see Mr and Mrs Ellis, and Tim and Zoe. We go back to Viking Hotel and God's your ankle!'

'Bob's your uncle,' corrected Mrs Tibblethwaite, before falling into silent thought. Go back to The Viking Hotel? Perhaps that would be the best thing to do – at least for the time being. Mind you, Sigurd was such a handful. He always seemed to bring trouble wherever he went. Mrs Tibblethwaite wondered what Mr and Mrs Ellis would think about the return of the Viking.

2 A Severe Case of Vikingitis

Zoe and Tim were delighted. They could not think of anything better than having Sigurd back at The Viking Hotel. They hurtled down the front steps of the hotel and launched themselves at the new guests.

'Tibby!' cried Zoe.

'Siggy!' yelled Tim.

'May the good Lord save us all,' murmured Mr Ellis to his pale wife.

He put on a brave smile and marched down the steps towards his uninvited guests. 'Sigurd – how nice to see you again after all this time. How are you?'

'How are you to you two too!' beamed Sigurd.

Tim burst out laughing. 'He sounds like an owl, doesn't he Zoe? Doesn't he sound like an owl? Too-wit, too-hoo, wooty-too, tooty-wooty-hooty . . .'

'All right, Tim,' said Mrs Ellis. 'I think we get the picture.' She turned to Mrs Tibblethwaite, took her suitcase from her and immediately ground to a halt because she couldn't manage the weight. Mrs Tibblethwaite picked it up with one hand. 'What's all this about?' asked Penny Ellis. 'This is a surprise.'

Mrs T. gave her a sharp look and nodded. 'I thought you might not be too pleased,' she sighed.

'Oh, it's not that . . .' Penny trailed off in confusion as her cheeks turned a delicate and embarrassed red. Mrs Tibblethwaite patted Penny's arm.

'It's quite all right. I thought you might be just a touch apprehensive about Siggy coming back here, but I'm afraid my dear that we had little choice.'

'We thought you were on another wrestling tour,' said Mrs Ellis.

'We were on a wrestling tour. Unfortunately things got a little out of hand at our last match . . .'

'How surprising,' murmured Penny, with a knowing glance at her friend. 'I don't suppose it had anything to do with Sigurd?'

'Of course it did, but it wasn't really his fault.'

'It hardly ever is,' Mrs Ellis pointed out. 'It's

just that he's always there when things go wrong.'

'Quite,' sighed Mrs Tibblethwaite. 'Anyway, to cut a long story short, we have been banned from wrestling in public ever again, so we are both out of a job. We didn't know what to do . . .'

'So you came here,' finished Penny and Mrs Tibblethwaite nodded glumly. 'Don't worry,' Penny went on brightly. 'You are very welcome – although I am not so sure about Siggy! Just look at him out in the garden with Tim and Keith.'

The two women peered out through the window. Sigurd seemed to be giving Tim lessons in swordsmanship. Tim was staggering round trying to lift Nosepicker above his head and going cross-eyed with the effort.

'You have to be like wild animal!' shouted Sigurd. 'You roar and stamp and scare your enemies! You rush at them and go Rraaaargh!'

'Sigurd,' interrupted Mr Ellis. 'Do you think you could look where you're going? You're treading on our new flowers. I only planted them last week.'

But Sigurd was far too busy showing Tim how fierce a real Viking warrior could be. 'I show you. You watch me. I scare panties on all enemies.'

'Siggy! You have to scare the pants off your enemies, not on them!' Tim giggled.

Sigurd seized Nosepicker from him. 'Raaargh!' he yelled, whirling the fierce blade round his head like a helicopter about to take off. 'Raaaargh!'

'Mind out!' cried Mr Ellis. 'You've just chopped my new forsythia bush in half!'

'Death to forsythia!' yelled Sigurd, taking another great swipe.

'It's only a bush, Siggy. It's not your deadly . . . argh! Help!' Mr Ellis suddenly set off round the garden as Sigurd leapt after him, growling and scowling and waving Nosepicker like a giant carving knife.

Round the garden they went, five times, until at last Sigurd stopped, put his hands on his hips and burst out laughing.

'You see me, Tim? I scare his panties all over the place.'

Mr Ellis collapsed exhausted on to the garden bench. His wife came out with a tray of tea and biscuits. 'Are you having fun, dear?' she asked gently. 'Playing Vikings with Siggy and Tim?' She winked at Mrs Tibblethwaite and Zoe. Poor Mr Ellis couldn't answer at first. He was too busy panting.

'That man's a maniac! He could have killed me! Will he be staying long? Oh I do hope not. I don't think I could cope. We've enough problems with the hotel as it is.'

'Oh please, Dad!' pleaded Zoe. 'Let him stay a bit. It's fun when Siggy's around.'

'Fun?! Look at this place! That Viking has only been here ten minutes and already the garden looks like the surface of the moon!'

'I'm afraid Siggy might be here for some time,' said Mrs Ellis. She handed him a cup of tea and explained about the wrestling ban. Her husband's face crumpled at the news. Mrs Tibblethwaite hastily reached inside her bag, pulled out a little silver flask and unscrewed the cap before offering it to Mr Ellis.

'Drink this. It's brandy – strictly for medicinal purposes. I usually have a drop or two when I find myself suffering from Vikingitis.'

Mr Ellis took a few gulps, coughed, spluttered and sat up straight. Colour flooded back to his face. The children watched him carefully.

'Please!' mouthed Zoe.

'You've got to let Sigurd stay or I shan't speak to you ever again!' scowled Tim.

'Is that a threat or a promise?' asked Mr Ellis. 'Okay, Siggy can stay for a while, but there are certain rules. Number one: no swords, indoors or outdoors. Number two: you both have to help in the hotel.'

'We'll do anything to help,' said Mrs Tibblethwaite.

'I help,' beamed Sigurd. 'You no want sword? Okey-dokey. I throw sword away!'

'Sigurd! No!'

But Sigurd had already hurled Nosepicker over one shoulder and the mighty sword was flying through the air. Five seconds later, there was an almighty crash of splintering glass as it smashed through the hotel greenhouse. Mr Ellis seized Mrs Tibblethwaite's silver hip-flask, took another deep swig and buried his head in both hands.

After that things quietened down a little. This was partly because Mr Ellis took to his bed with a headache and various other symptoms of Vikingitis, while Mrs Tibblethwaite and Siggy got settled into one of the hotel bedrooms.

The only other guests at the hotel were an

elderly couple, the Ramsbottoms, and Mr Travis, who was in Flotby on business. The truth of the matter was that since Sigurd had left business had gone down. While there had been a real tenth-century Viking staying at the hotel it had attracted customers. But when Siggy and Tibby became a tag-wrestling team and began their country-wide tour many of the hotel guests left, and had not returned.

The Viking Hotel was beginning to look a bit tatty. What it really needed was a good coat of paint. The Ellises had already decided they ought to do the painting while there were so few guests staying and Mr Ellis reckoned that Sigurd could make himself useful with a paintbrush. Early the next day he set the Viking to the task. 'Do the front of the house first of all,' said Mr Ellis, leaning a ladder against the front porch. 'I want all the doors done, and the windows and the railings. Understand?'

'Okey-dokey, boss,' nodded Sigurd, levering the lid off the paint tin. There was a loud SCROYYOINNGG! and the lid whizzed across the road like a flying saucer and landed upside down on Mr Crump's front doorstep. Mr Ellis sighed and went back inside.

Sigurd quickly warmed to his task. The paint was a lovely bright green. Up and down the ladder he went, singing away to himself one of the songs Tim had taught him, but with new words.

'Siggy Viking had a brush;
slip-slap, slip-slap-slop!
And on this brush
he had some paint;
slip-slap, slip-slap-slop!
With a plip-plop here
and a plip-plop there –
Here a plip!
There a plop!
Everywhere a plip-plop!
Siggy Viking had a . . .'

'SIGGY WHAT ON EARTH ARE YOU DOING?' Mrs Ellis stood on the pavement gazing up at the front of the hotel in disbelief. There was bright green paint everywhere.

Sigurd had spilled great green puddles all over the entrance. Then he had walked in the puddles and left bright green bootprints up and down the porch. There were bright green handprints all over the walls. Most of Sigurd's helmet was bright green, and so were his clothes. He grinned down at Mrs Ellis.

'I go painting,' he said proudly. 'With a plip-plop here and a . . .'

'But you've painted all the windows!' yelled Mrs Ellis, almost beside herself.

'Mr Ellis said paint the doors and the railings and the windows,' nodded Sigurd.

'BUT YOU'VE PAINTED ALL THE GLASS!' screamed Mrs Ellis. 'All our windows are bright green. Nobody can see out anymore – Mr and Mrs Ramsbottom think it's still night-time and won't come down for breakfast!'

On the other side of the road Mr Crump opened his front door to see what all the fuss was about and stepped straight on to an upturned lid of bright green paint. He boggled at the shining green hotel opposite, shook his foot angrily and sent the paint-lid skimming back along his hall, where it left a nice green skid trail the entire length of the carpet. Mrs Ellis took one look at his angry face, ran inside, bolted the door and rushed upstairs to the bedroom. Another very severe case of Vikingitis had just taken hold.

3 Let's all be Friends!

It was an impossible task. The green paint stuck
to the glass like glue and no matter what the
Ellises tried they could not get the paint off.
Eventually Mr Ellis had to call out some
decorators. The glass had to be removed from the
window frames and replaced. The decorators had
to re-do all the painting properly and then they
presented Mr Ellis with a big bill for the work. He
was not very pleased, although he did blame
himself for what had happened.

'I had forgotten just how stupid Sigurd can
be,' he muttered.

'You did tell him to paint the windows,' Zoe
pointed out. 'So he did.'

'Thank you, Zoe, for that helpful comment,'
Mr Ellis replied icily.

Mrs Ellis folded her arms. 'We are going to
have to do something, Keith. We can't have Sigurd
ruining everything we've worked so hard for.'

'I know. If only we could think of a way to
get him out of the hotel most of the time. At least
he wouldn't be under our feet then. Tim and Zoe

go to school, which gets them out of the way. It's a shame Sigurd is too old for school.' His voice trailed away and a faint wisp of a smile flickered across his face. 'We can't get him into school, can we?'

'He is a bit big for Playgroup, which is where he should be,' Mrs Ellis admitted. 'He'd love Playgroup – all that sand and water . . .'

'And paint,' added Mr Ellis. 'They always do lots of painting.'

'The trouble is, I think the school would notice. Imagine Siggy arriving for the day. He'd be standing there in his school uniform, with his bent helmet rammed on his head and Nosepicker by his side . . .' Penny Ellis began to laugh. 'No, I'm afraid he's too big for school.'

'He can come to school with me,' said Tim, poking his head round the door. 'The other children would think it was brill.'

'Brill? Who taught you to speak like that?' asked Mr Ellis.

'Speak like what?' asked Tim. 'Anyway, Siggy can come in with me tomorrow. Mr Rumble will like that.'

'I doubt it,' murmured Mrs Ellis. 'I don't think it's a good idea, Tim.'

'Oh go on,' pleaded Tim. 'Everyone else brings things in. James brought in his rabbit last week, and Rachel Wagstaff had an eskimo doll made out of whalebone and sealskin.'

'Yes, but a real person is rather different,' said Mrs Ellis, still shaking her head.

'A real person is even better,' pronounced Tim. 'People can see rabbits any day they want and anyway it did a poo on James' desk. And the doll was boring and the sealskin stank. A real Viking would be brilliant. Siggy can tell the whole class about what it was like in Viking times, and Mr Rumble will like it 'cos he always does when people bring things in 'cos he doesn't have to do so much teaching, and Siggy won't do poos like the rabbit and he doesn't stink either – well, not much anyway.'

Tim's parents listened to this long speech with growing astonishment. 'Good grief,' said his father. 'I didn't know you had so many words inside you, Tim.'

'I've got billions of words inside me,' Tim explained. 'But most of the time I think them rather than say them. Sometimes when I say things it comes out all wrong, only it didn't just then. The words all came out right.'

Mr Ellis laughed. 'They certainly did.'

'So can Siggy come into school with me then?'

Mrs Ellis nodded. 'We'll give it a try, Tim. But he had better behave himself. Go and tell him. He's upstairs. Mrs Tibblethwaite locked him in their room to make sure he didn't cause any more damage.' Tim vanished in a flash and a moment later the Ellises heard the sound of his feet charging up the stairs.

'Strange how one pair of feet can sound like a whole herd of dinosaurs,' mused Mrs Ellis. 'I hope we've made the right decision, Keith.'

'Put it this way,' said Mr Ellis. 'Tomorrow Siggy will be out of our hair almost the whole day. I can't think of anything better.'

Tim and Zoe both felt extremely proud the next day. They walked into school on either side of Siggy, holding his hands. The children and teachers all knew about Sigurd of course. Many of them had seen him when he went shopping in Flotby with the Ellises, but it was quite different to have him in their school. A real Viking in their school!

Most of the boys wanted Sigurd to get out

Nosepicker and do some swordfighting but Zoe
was very sensible and managed to prevent a
major disaster in the playground. 'We'll show
them later, Sigurd,' she said. Then there was a bit
of a scuffle because they all wanted to try on his
helmet. And finally Zoe and Tim had a quarrel
over whose class Sigurd would go to first, and
Tim won, because it had been his idea.

At Assembly Mrs Crock, the head teacher,
introduced Sigurd to the whole school. Mrs
Crock was a slim, small lady, with neat grey hair
fixed in a bun. She always stood on a little box to
talk to the children, but, even so, she was still
shorter than Sigurd.

The Viking stood next to her with his black
hair exploding from beneath his battered helmet,
and a fierce smile on his face.

'Children,' began Mrs Crock. 'We are
delighted to have Sigurd the Viking with us this
week. He will be telling you what it was like to
be a Viking and everything about Viking life.
Sigurd is an important visitor, so please look
after him well. Sigurd, would you like to say
something?'

Sigurd stepped forward and beamed at
everyone in the hall. 'I Sigurd. I come from

Hedeby, Denmark. How do I do and the same to you.' He pointed round the big room. 'This cruel. I like cruel.' Mrs Crock nudged him gently.

'School,' she hissed.

'Yes – scrool!' said Sigurd cheerfully. 'Scrool good place. You learn much things. I teach you Viking things. I make you good Vikings. Now I say cheerio and shake your hands and goodbye Mrs Crocodile.' Sigurd turned to the head teacher, threw his arms round her, gave her an enormous, loud kiss on each cheek and then rubbed his nose against hers. 'There!'

Mrs Crock almost fell from her wooden box. She stood there rocking back on her feet, quite speechless, while Sigurd grinned at everyone. 'That old Viking custom,' he said. 'You watch. I show you again,' and before Mrs Crock could escape she found herself captured in the Viking's hairy arms once again. 'Now everyone try,' cried Sigurd. 'Everybody stand up. You go to person next to you . . .'

Nobody moved. The teachers stared back at him, aghast, as their head teacher fainted, and slowly sank to the floor. The children watched and hoped they didn't really have to do all this hugging and kissing and nose-rubbing, but Sigurd was adamant. He whipped out Nosepicker and brandished it furiously above his head.

'Everybody stand up!' he ordered. 'Now you put arms round necks, hugsy-wugsy, and kiss on chops, slopsy-wopsy, then rub noses, grotty-snotty.'

The hall was an extraordinary sight. Two hundred and thirty children began shouting and grappling with each other. Eight teachers turned red with embarrassment and began hugging one another.

'You be very careful, Mr Rumble,' warned Mrs Blatt. 'My husband is a policeman.'

'You be careful,' he answered coldly, 'or I shall have to report you to him.'

From the children came a great moan of disgust. Even Tim and Zoe were unsure of this Viking custom.

'Urgh! You kissed me, Zoe!'

'Well I tried not to. Do you think I wanted to kiss you? You should have kept your face out of the way. I shall probably get the plague now.'

'Yuk! Get your nose off me!' shouted Rachel Wagstaff to some poor five year old, who immediately burst into tears.

Sigurd was very pleased, and he stood there

grinning at everyone. He didn't seem to notice
that several fights had now broken out between
the children, and between the teachers too. Those
that weren't fighting or arguing were crying.
They didn't like this Viking custom at all.

'Now we all good friends!' Sigurd declared,
ignoring the fact that the hall was a wriggling
mass of squealing bodies, all trying to escape. He
bent down, picked up the unconscious Mrs Crock
and threw her over one shoulder. He knew just
how to bring her round.

Sigurd marched off down the corridor with
the head teacher dangling over his shoulder. He
poked his head round every door and at last
found a wash-room. He propped Mrs Crock up
on the tiled floor, filled a nearby mop bucket with
cold water and poured the entire contents over
the hapless head.

Mrs Crock jerked, gulped, coughed,
spluttered and opened her eyes. Her hair
straggled down her face and shoulders and her
make-up trickled down her cheeks, making long,
blue-black smudges. She sat there in an enormous
pool of water and stared up at the Viking who
was busily refilling his bucket.

'Noooooo! Keep away from me!' she

shouted. She leapt to her feet and was off down the corridor at top squelching speed.

'Mrs Crocodile all right now,' Sigurd said to himself as he watched her vanish with great satisfaction. He had been in school for less than half an hour, and already he had reduced the place to a shambles.

4 All at Sea

Sigurd and Tim and Zoe stood in the head teacher's office looking across at Mrs Crock. 'I think we got off to a bad start,' said the head teacher. One of the cooks from the school kitchen had kindly lent the head teacher a cook's uniform, so that she had something dry to wear. Mrs Crock's hair was still rather bedraggled, and she had poked it up underneath a cook's cap. Tim was very surprised to see Mrs Crock in a blue uniform.

'Are you going to do the cooking today, Mrs Crock?' Zoe, who knew exactly why Mrs Crock was dressed like a cook, nudged her brother, but it was too late. Mrs Crock fixed him with a steely glare.

'No, Tim, I am not going to do the cooking today. I am wearing this uniform because . . . because I wet my dress earlier and I had to change.'

Tim's eyes almost popped out of his head. 'You wet yourself!' he whispered in awe. Mrs Crock went very red.

'Of course I didn't! Don't be so stupid!
I meant that my dress became wet. In fact it was
soaked, by your Viking friend here.' Now the
head teacher glared at Sigurd, and he shrugged.

'I try to help,' he explained.

Mrs Crock sighed. 'I know. I understand that
it was a mistake. However, if you are going to
visit the classrooms today then I must ask you to
make sure that you do not make the children, or
the teachers, do anything silly: like all that
ridiculous kissing and hugging.'

'Viking custom,' growled Sigurd.

'Yes, I know it's a Viking custom. But we are
not Vikings. We are civilised human beings.'

Sigurd frowned. 'Scoose me,' he said. 'What
is silly-fly human bean?'

'Oh never mind.' Poor Mrs Crock felt totally
exhausted, and it was only a quarter to ten. 'Tim,
take Sigurd to your class, and please, please make
sure he doesn't do anything stupid.'

'I not stupid,' Sigurd protested.

'Of course you're not,' smiled Mrs Crock,
showing them the door and closing it behind
them. 'You're just a complete and utter nutcase,'
she muttered to herself before collapsing into a
chair. Wearily she pulled open a little drawer in

her desk and got out a small, silver hip-flask. It was astonishing how many people in Flotby had hip-flasks. Sales were on the increase now that Sigurd was back in town.

Sigurd squeezed himself into the chair next to Tim, just managing to get his knees under the table. Tim grinned at his classmates, and they stared back at the great big hairy Viking sitting in their classroom. Mr Rumble smiled.

'We are very lucky this morning, children. Tim's friend Sigurd is going to tell us about Viking times. I shall sit down in this quiet corner. Sigurd – why don't you come to the front of the class?'

The Viking beamed with pleasure and got up. Unfortunately his knees were still jammed under the table which overbalanced and crashed to the floor. Rachel Wagstaff sniggered.

'He's very clumsy for a Viking,' she murmured. 'I bet he's not a real Viking. He's just pretend.'

'He is real!' hissed Tim, as he put the table back on its legs. 'And you can shut up, Rachel.'

Rachel's hand shot into the air and waved about madly. 'Mr Rumble, Tim told me to shut up!'

'Good idea,' thought Mr Rumble, but he smiled and said, 'Over to you, Sigurd. What are you going to tell us about?'

Sigurd took off his helmet, scratched his head, put his helmet back on and stared at his feet. 'I Viking!' he announced.

'Yes, we know that,' sighed Mr Rumble.

'I Sigurd, from Hedeby, Denmark.'

'Yes. We know that too.'

'I fierce warrior.' Sigurd pulled his fiercest face and Mandy Perkins screamed. Mandy Perkins was always screaming about something.

'He's only pretending,' Tim pointed out with a groan.

'It's all right, Mandy, Sigurd is acting,' explained Mr Rumble. He turned to the Viking. 'Tell us about life in Hedeby, Sigurd.'

'Hedeby – my town. Lots of Vikings: some big like me, some small like baby, some young like Tim, some old like Crumble . . .'

'Rumble!' snapped Mr Rumble. 'And I'm not that old either, if you don't mind. What did you eat?'

Sigurd closed his eyes and licked his lips. 'Sometimes we have big feet,' he said. 'Very big feet to praise Thor, God of Thunder.'

'He means feast,' whispered Tim to the rest of the class, who were beginning to giggle.

'We eat chickens and pigs and sheets and coats.'

'Sheep and goats,' muttered Tim.

'I don't think people should eat meat,' said Rachel. 'I'm a vegetarian.' Sigurd scowled, leant over Rachel's table and put one hand on Nosepicker.

'Vikings kill vegetables,' he hissed.

'Oh!' squeaked Rachel, and she didn't say anything else for a long time.

After that things went quite well for a while. The children became engrossed in what Sigurd told them and they began asking questions. Tim sat back proudly and listened to his tenth-century friend and Mr Rumble dozed quietly in the corner. It was when Terry Reeves started asking about Viking longships that things began to go wrong – again. Terry wanted to know how everyone knew when to row.

'I went in a rowing boat with my dad once,' he said. 'I had two oars and he had two oars but we couldn't put them in the water at the same time. We just went round and round until he bashed one of my oars with his oar and they both broke and we got told off and had to be rescued.'

Sigurd nodded; this was a problem he knew well. He was hopeless at rowing himself but he would never admit it. In fact, he pretended he was pretty good at it. 'I show you how we row,' he declared. 'First we put tables on sides like this.' He made two rows of tables down the classroom, with their legs pointing inwards. 'Now you put cheese down middle.'

'Cheese?' repeated Terry. 'I haven't got any cheese.'

'I've got some cheese in my sandwich,' James said. 'But that's for my lunch.'

'I think he might mean chairs,' Tim suggested.

'Cheese!' grinned Sigurd, picking up one chair after another, and putting them in rows of four between the tables. 'Now we get oars.'

Tim stared at the tables and chairs. 'Siggy's made a longship!' he cried. 'Look, the tables are the sides of the boat and the chairs are the benches that the rowers sit on. Brill – I'll get some oars! James – you come with me, and Terry.' The three boys dashed out of the classroom, while Mr Rumble snored away in the corner, dreaming about being a Viking.

A few moments later Tim and the others came racing back. They had raided the caretaker's cupboard and taken a whole assortment of long-handled brooms, mops, window-openers and anything that was long, thin and vaguely oar-like.

'Now you take oars!' cried Siggy. The children settled into their seats and seized their oars. 'We go Hedeby! Oars forward!'

Fourteen assorted mops, brooms and window-openers waved in the air. Several flowerpots were knocked from the windowsill on the port side, while on the starboard bow a rack of newly-filled paint-pots crashed to the floor and began making a multicoloured ocean for the longship to sail across.

Sigurd had never seen such hopeless rowing. He leapt on to Mr Rumble's desk and pulled Nosepicker from its tatty scabbard. 'You keep time with me!' he roared, beating out a rowing rhythm on Mr Rumble's desk with Nosepicker's heavy blade. 'In! Out! In! Out!' Large chips of wood splintered off the desk and spun through the air.

The longship was beginning to sink. The rowers were all quarrelling because they kept hitting each other with their brooms and mops. Mandy Perkins started screaming. Sally threw a flowerpot at Adam because she thought he'd flicked her with paint and Terry pushed Tim overboard.

Sigurd jumped up and down so much that he managed to jam the horns of his helmet into one of the overhead light fittings and rip it from the ceiling. He couldn't quite keep his balance with a large fluorescent light fitting waving about on his helmet and after a few seconds, he went tumbling down into Mr Rumble's lap.

'Eh! Eh! EH!' cried Mr Rumble, scrambling out from beneath Sigurd. He gazed round his classroom. Children were crawling through a mixed-up sea of paint, mud and flowers and prodding each other with mops and brooms. Plaster trickled down from the ceiling where Sigurd had ripped out the light, and now the Viking was on his feet and striding round the classroom, still with a light tube stuck on his helmet and shouting 'In! Out! In! Out!'

Mr Rumble joined in. 'Out! Out! Out!' he bellowed, seizing a window-pole and poking Sigurd. 'Get out of my classroom at once! You're not a Viking – you're a disaster!' And with one final, vicious prod he sent Sigurd scampering up the corridor.

It was now almost twelve o'clock and Sigurd had reduced the school to a shambles a second time.

5   A Viking all Alone

At lunch time, Mrs Crock took Sigurd home. She had taken one look at Mr Rumble's shipwrecked classroom and decided it was the best thing to do. Zoe and Tim went with her to keep an eye on Sigurd.

Mr and Mrs Ellis were not surprised to see Sigurd being frog-marched up the hotel steps by Mrs Crock, but they were rather bemused by the cook's uniform the head teacher was wearing. Zoe noticed both her parents staring.

'It's a long story,' she began.

'It's a wet story,' Tim added.

Mrs Crock only stopped long enough to make a brief announcement. 'If this Viking comes anywhere near my school ever again, I shall kill him,' she said bluntly. 'I shall probably strangle him with my bare hands. I might even slice him up on my paper-trimmer and put the bits in a thousand different files in my filing cabinet.'

'Things didn't work out, then?' offered Mr Ellis.

'That, Mr Ellis, is an understatement.' Mrs

Crock turned on her heels and strode back to the car. The door slammed, the engine revved and with a great deal of wheelspin Mrs Crock vanished.

'Wow! Can she drive!' breathed Tim.

There was a long, cold, silent pause while everyone stood on the hotel steps. Sigurd tried a helpful smile, and his dark eyes shot from one Ellis to another. Even Tim could sense that there was trouble ahead – big trouble. He felt for his sister's hand and together they slipped quietly into the hotel. They hid behind the front door and listened, desperate to know what was going to happen.

Mr and Mrs Ellis stood across the hotel doorway, blocking the entrance. 'You can't come in,' said Mr Ellis. 'I'm sorry, Sigurd, but we're not having you back here. Every time you turn up there is trouble. We cannot afford to keep paying for the mistakes you make and we are not prepared to let you live in our hotel any longer. You've got to go. Mrs Tibblethwaite can stay here until she finds somewhere more suitable. In the meantime you will just have to manage for yourself.'

Tim and Zoe came racing out from behind

the front door. 'Dad! Mum! You can't throw him out!'

'Oh yes we can,' said Mrs Ellis. 'It might seem cruel to you, but Sigurd has to go. He has cost us hundreds, probably thousands of pounds. He has driven everyone mad. Your father and I cannot cope any longer. We have enough worries trying to run this hotel, especially with business so bad at present.'

'But throwing him out!' Zoe cried. 'It's not right. He'll be homeless.'

'I've thought of that,' said Mr Ellis. 'He can stay in the greenhouse until Mrs Tibblethwaite finds somewhere better for him.'

'The greenhouse? But Dad, half the glass is broken.'

'I know. Sigurd was the one who broke it, so that's his problem. Come on, everyone inside, the Ramsbottoms are waiting for their lunch.' Mr Ellis pushed his children into the hotel with Mrs Ellis following hard on their heels. She turned on the doorstep and eyed Sigurd sternly.

'You've made all these problems, Siggy,' she said. 'Just for once, you sort them out.'

She stepped inside and shut the door, leaning back against it, her face white and drawn. She was certain that this was the hardest thing she had ever done in her life; but it had to be done. Somehow Sigurd had to understand his responsibilities to other people.

Sigurd stood on the hotel porch, gazing at the closed door. All his friends, all the people he most loved, were on the other side of that door, shut away from him. He backed slowly down the hotel steps, his eyes fixed on the front of The Viking Hotel, but the door didn't open. Then he turned and walked away.

Tim and Zoe sat on Zoe's bed with their backs to the wall and their knees hunched up against their chests. 'The thing is,' said Zoe, 'Siggy could be out there anywhere. Anything might have happened to him by now.'

'He could have been kidnapped,' suggested Tim.

'Yeah . . .' said Zoe, although she couldn't imagine why anyone in their right mind would want to kidnap a smelly, dirty Viking warrior like Sigurd.

'He might have had all his blood sucked out by Dracula,' Tim continued. Zoe thought that this was also rather unlikely.

'Or chewed to bits by a werewolf, or

snatched from the planet by aliens with three heads and ten legs . . .'

'Tim!'

Tim frowned to himself and counted carefully on his fingers before turning to his sister. 'Zoe, if you have ten legs does that mean you must have five bottoms?'

'TIM! What are we going to do about Siggy?'

'It's Dad's fault,' muttered Tim through his teeth.

'And Mum's,' Zoe added. 'They should be arrested and taken to court and charged with um . . .' Zoe couldn't quite decide what her parents ought to be charged with.

'Cruelty to Vikings,' suggested Tim.

'Yeah, something like that.' There was a short silence during which Tim gave up trying to think for himself.

'Maybe we could smuggle him back into the hotel,' Zoe murmured.

'Smuggle him back in? Brilliant idea! We could hide him in my room!'

'I don't think that would work, Tim. The best place for him would be one of the empty guest rooms.'

'You can be quite clever sometimes, for
a girl.'

Zoe glanced up at her brother's smiling face.
'And you can be quite stupid,' she replied. 'Most
of the time.' Tim's smile vanished.

'That's not very nice,' he grumbled. She
grinned and grabbed hold of his hand.

'Come on. Let's see if we can find Siggy.
He'll probably be down on the beach somewhere.
He always goes and stares at the sea when he's
upset about something.'

'How do you know?' asked Tim, who had
never noticed anything of the sort.

'Because I'm a girl and I'm clever.'

Tim had no answer to this. It was a real pain
being two years younger than his sister. It meant
that Zoe was always two years older. She was
always ahead of him. He would never, ever be
able to catch her up. Life was very unfair.

Zoe was right, too. Sigurd was down on the
beach, standing at the water's edge and staring
out at the flat, grey shimmering sea, while little
waves rolled up to his feet and frothed over
them. The children went and stood quietly at
his side.

'Siggy?' Zoe held his big hand.

'Mmmmm?''

'What are you thinking?'

'I think Sigurd stupid,' growled the Viking. 'He biggest stupid in whole world.'

'No you're not!' cried Tim.

'More stupid than donkey; more stupid than dog; even more stupid than eeny-weeny-teeny-titchy-witchy-snitchy mouse.'

'No you're not!' Tim repeated. Sigurd gave a big gloomy sigh and threw a stone into the sea.

'I more stupid than carrot,' he announced sadly.

Zoe felt that the conversation was rapidly slipping into a list of animals and vegetables. Sigurd could probably keep up this display of self-pity for hours. 'Listen, Tim and I have got an idea. We could smuggle you back into the hotel.'

'Scoose me, what is smuggle?'

'We sneak you into the hotel when no one's looking, and you can hide in one of the spare rooms.'

Sigurd picked up another stone and hurled it as far as he could. The stone seemed to curve through the air for ages before at last it dived down into the distant sea. A burst of foam exploded into the air, marking where the stone hit the surface, before it vanished from sight. Sigurd turned to Zoe and shook his head.

'No,' he said firmly. 'I no go smuggling and sneaking. Mr, Mrs Ellis – they very angry with Sigurd. They right. I bad man.'

'You're not bad!' protested Zoe. 'You're just, sort of, different.'

'I make mess,' Sigurd went on. 'I break things, make people cross. I no good in hotel. I good one thing only – make trouble. Trouble easy-peasy for me. People say – Sigurd, what you do? I say I do trouble. I do good trouble. You want big trouble, small trouble, or piddle-size trouble?'

'Sigurd,' pleaded Zoe. 'Don't go on like that. Please come back to the hotel.'

But the Viking pulled his big hand away from hers. 'Go home, Tim. Go home, Zoe. I find place to sleep. Maybe I go to bluehouse like Mr Ellis say.'

'Greenhouse,' said Tim. 'Not bluehouse.'

Sigurd shrugged. 'Greenhouse, bluehouse – it good place for man like carrot. You clever – hotel your house. Now I stay here alone. Want to think.'

Tim and Zoe trudged back across the wet

sand without him. 'He's not really as stupid as a carrot, is he?' asked Tim.

'Of course he isn't. He's just feeling a bit sorry for himself.'

'And he isn't trouble either, is he?'

Zoe thought for a few moments before answering. 'Well, he is a bit,' she said. 'Really.' She walked several steps and then spoke again. 'I think that's why I like him so much.'

6 With a Mud-pat Here, and a Cow-pat There . . .

Tim and Zoe pleaded with their parents all evening, but it was no use. Even Mrs Tibblethwaite thought that Mr and Mrs Ellis had done the right thing. 'I would have thrown him out long ago,' she said.

'How can you say that?' shouted Zoe. 'You're married to him. You're supposed to love him!'

'Just because you love someone, Zoe, it doesn't mean that you have to put up with everything they do. I do love Siggy, but most of the time he's like an enormous child. He has to learn how to behave.'

'Why?' asked Tim.

'Because that is what all people have to do, even tenth-century Vikings.'

'Huh!' Tim didn't think much of this at all. Zoe felt the same way as her brother, but she tried to put her feelings into proper words.

'People like Siggy because he's different,' she said. 'They like him because he doesn't behave the way the rest of us have to. That's what makes him such fun.'

Mrs Ellis managed a faint smile. 'I'm sure you're right, Zoe, but you have to admit that it is difficult for us. It's all right for other people to laugh at Siggy's stupid mistakes; they don't have to pick up the pieces and pay for the damage, or live with him day by day. We do.'

'You won't let him back in then?' Tim asked.

'No,' said Mr Ellis. 'Sorry.'

'Then I shall never speak to you again and I'm going on strike.'

'But you don't do anything,' Mr Ellis pointed out.

'A hunger strike,' Tim said, glaring at his parents. 'I shan't eat anything until you let Siggy back into the hotel.' Hah! They'd soon change their minds now!

'Fine,' said Mrs Ellis. 'That should save us some money on food bills at any rate.'

'You'll let me starve?' cried Tim.

Mr Ellis shook his head. 'Of course not, Tim. We wouldn't let you starve. We'll let you eat any time. You're starving yourself.' Tim clenched his fists. This was too much. He'd been out-argued again.

He leapt to his feet and stamped out of the room. Zoe watched him go.

'Now look what you've done!' she cried, and ran from the room in tears.

Mr and Mrs Ellis glanced across at Mrs Tibblethwaite. 'Oh dear,' said Mrs Ellis. 'It is hard.'

'Hard for everyone,' agreed Mrs T. 'But don't worry. I'm sure things will turn out all right in the end. Tim won't go for long without eating.'

'Oh I know that,' said Mrs Ellis. 'It's Zoe I'm worried about.'

Mrs Tibblethwaite reached forward and patted Mrs Ellis on the hand. 'Zoe is a clever girl, and sensitive too. I'm sure she understands really, and that's why it upsets her so much. Siggy will be all right. Goodness, he must have spent hundreds of nights outside, sleeping under the stars when he was a proper Viking in proper Viking times. I wouldn't worry about him at all. Goodnight!'

Tim stuck to his guns. He refused supper and he turned down a drink and a biscuit before bedtime. By the time he crawled into bed he was starving. His stomach was aching for food and he cursed himself for saying that he was on hunger strike. He tossed and turned for hours and was just drifting off to sleep when he heard the bedroom door open. Zoe quickly slipped into the room and shut the door. She tiptoed across to the bed.

'Are you awake?'

'Of course I'm awake. My stomach is making very loud empty noises. I can't sleep.'

'I've brought you some food,' Zoe whispered, and she pulled two chunky sandwiches from inside her dressing-gown. 'That one's got a bit of fluff on it, I'm afraid. I had to hide them under here.'

'That's okay,' said Tim, stuffing it into his mouth. 'I like fluff sandwiches. Thanks. I was starving.'

'I knew you would be. Anyway, it was very brave of you to go on hunger strike.'

'Yeah? Yeah! It was. I could have died.'

'Tim – you've only been without food for about ten hours,' laughed Zoe.

'Ten hours? It feels more like ten months.'

Zoe sat down on the edge of Tim's bed. 'I'll try and get something for you tomorrow at breakfast. Mr Travis always leaves his toast and . . .' Zoe stopped in mid-sentence, frowned and went across to the window. She pulled back the curtains a little way and peered into the darkness. 'Did you hear something?' she asked her brother.

'No. Did you?' Tim slipped out of bed and joined Zoe at the window. Now they could both hear odd sounds from outside. Bumping, banging and dragging noises drifted up from the back garden of the hotel.

'Is that someone humming?' asked Tim.

'I don't know,' Zoe answered, 'but I think I just saw a pig.'

'A pig! Don't be daft!'

'Well it looked like a pig,' Zoe insisted.

'It could have been a werewolf,' whispered her brother, his eyes growing bigger and bigger. 'Or a ghost.'

'It was a pig,' repeated Zoe.

'Maybe it was ghost-pig,' Tim went on. 'The Ghastly Ghost-Pig of Flotby. Or maybe even a were-pig-wolf-ghost-thingy . . .'

'A were-ghost-pig-wolf-whotsit?'

'Yeah – with fangs that shine in the dark and X-ray eyes and stuff . . .'

Zoe pulled the curtains back into place and

summoned up her courage. 'Well, whatever it is, there's something going on out there. I'm going downstairs to see what it is.'

'And I'm coming with you,' said Tim, who suddenly felt that he didn't want to be left alone. He grabbed his torch.

The two children crept silently down the back stairs and tiptoed out through the hotel kitchen. Zoe quietly unlocked the back door. The noises were much louder now – grunts and squeaks and bangs and thuds. Zoe felt for Tim's hand. 'Are you scared?' she whispered.

'No,' lied Tim. 'Are you?'

'Yes, a bit.'

'Then I am too,' Tim decided. They pressed forward across the path and on to the dark lawn, moving slowly towards the source of all the noise. They had just reached the nearest corner of the greenhouse when a huge, dark figure loomed right in front of them, giving the children the most enormous fright.

'Aargh!' screamed Tim, dropping his torch and running like mad across the lawn. 'It's the were-ghost!'

'Aaargh!' screamed Zoe, racing off in the other direction. 'It's a pig-wolf!'

'Aaaargh!' bellowed Sigurd, dropping a large pile of sticks and drawing Nosepicker. 'It's rubbers! You bad peoples – come to rub hotel. I kill rubbers!'

Tim stopped running and looked back at the Viking. 'I'm not a rubber, I mean robber,' he said crossly. 'I'm Tim.'

Sigurd stopped poking the night air with Nosepicker and calmed down. 'You give me fright,' he told Tim and Zoe.

'You gave us a fright!' said Zoe. 'But I'm glad you're all right, Siggy. What are you doing out here?'

Sigurd slipped Nosepicker back into its scabbard. His white teeth flashed a moonlit grin. 'I show you. I stand on beach and think very hard. Tide coming in. Water come up to my knees. I still thinking what to do. Water come to tummy. I still think. Water come to neck. Think I drown so get out of sea and walk down road. Then I have pig idea.'

'Big idea,' corrected Zoe.

'No,' said Sigurd. 'Pig idea. Look.'

Sigurd led the children over to the far corner of the hotel garden. Siggy had made a kind of pen. He had banged wooden posts into the ground and woven branches in between the posts. He had covered the branches with some kind of muddy mixture that was still drying. And on the other side of the pen were three extremely large pigs. They gazed sleepily at Tim and Zoe. One gave a quiet 'oink'.

'You did all this?' murmured Zoe admiringly. 'It's called wattle and daub, isn't it? I didn't know you could make fences, Siggy.'

'Vikings always make fences like this. Put in post, bang-bang. Put in branches. Mix up mud and straw and cow-stuff . . .'

'Cow-stuff?' Tim repeated, not sure if he wanted to hear about how to make a wattle and daub fence.

'They mixed in cow-pats as well,' explained Zoe.

'Urgh, that's revolting!' cried Tim. Sigurd shook his head.

'I no find cows. No cow-stuff, but good fence anyway.'

'Where did the pigs come from?' asked Zoe.

'I find them.'

'You found three pigs?'

It was very dark, so Tim and Zoe couldn't see how red Sigurd had gone. He went back to the greenhouse to collect the pile of wood he had dropped. 'Actually, I find four pigs, walking down road, but one run away, trit-trot. She big pig. Very big pig. She big bad pig. You see pig?'

'No, we no see pig – I mean we didn't see a pig anywhere,' replied Zoe.

'Never mind. Now I build house for Sigurd,' said the Viking, and he began banging in a row of tall posts. 'Hotel too smart for Viking. I make Viking house in garden. Take long time. You go bed. I see you in . . .'

'Eeeeeek!'

'Aaaargh!'

Startled screams from the hotel interrupted Sigurd in mid-sentence. A bedroom window flew open and the children watched, astonished, as their parents clambered out at top speed, as if the hotel was on fire.

Mrs Ellis managed to grab hold of the thick ivy running up one side of the window frame, but Mr Ellis was left dangling from the window ledge by his fingertips. A few seconds later there was a loud and angry grunt and a huge sow shoved her trotters up on the window sill and peered out, snorting and sniffing like a flesh-eating ogre. 'Help! Help!' cried Mr Ellis. 'Someone save us! There's a giant pig in our bedroom!'

7 Three Cheers for Sigurd!

Sigurd leapt to the rescue. He grabbed a ladder
from behind the greenhouse and dashed across to
the hotel. Penny Ellis had managed to clamber
down the ivy, but her husband was still hanging
by his fingernails. In a flash Siggy had raced up
the ladder and plucked Mr Ellis from the window
ledge. He flung him over his shoulder and quickly
backed down the ladder, while the murderous pig
began shredding the Ellis's best velvet curtains
with its vicious teeth.

'Sigurd, you saved my life,' panted Mr Ellis.
'I'm very grateful to you, but what do we do now?
The pig's already eaten one of the hall rugs,
several pot plants and that lovely painting we had
of Flotby harbour.'

'Where did the pig come from anyway?'
asked Mrs Ellis. 'Is this anything to do with you,
Sigurd?'

'It wasn't his fault,' Tim blurted out. 'Siggy
found them, on the road.'

'Them?' repeated Mr Ellis. 'Please don't tell

me there are some more? And how can you find a pig on the road? That's ridiculous.'

Zoe pulled her parents over to Sigurd's pig pen. Mr and Mrs Ellis stared at the three sleepy occupants. 'Siggy made this,' explained Zoe. 'Isn't he clever? It's a wattle and daub fence, and now he's making a little house too – look.'

'Don't change the subject, Zoe. Where did the pigs come from? You don't find pigs just walking down the road as if they were off to do their shopping,' snapped Mr Ellis.

Sigurd burst out laughing. 'Pig do shopping! Ha ha! Very good! Very funny! This little piggy go to market!'

'They're not little piggies at all, Sigurd. They're the biggest piggies I have ever seen. You stole them didn't you? You stole them from the farm up near the cliffs.'

Sigurd's smile vanished and he shook his head seriously. 'I no steal! I find on road. I walk up road. Pig walk down road. One, two, three, four pig. I say, "Hallo pig! You come walkies with me. I make you nice home." Pig follow me. I come here and make fence for pig but one run away. She very big, like dragon. It dark. I no see where she go. Maybe she hungry. Maybe she go hotel. Now she eat curtains.'

Zoe tugged anxiously at the Viking's sleeve. 'Siggy, I think Mrs Tibblethwaite is still in there,' she whispered. Mr Ellis gave a despairing cry.

'So are Mr Travis and the Ramsbottoms!'

'No fear, Sigurd here!' roared the Viking, and he whipped out Nosepicker. He brandished the great sword high above his head and struck his most heroic pose. 'Now I catch pig and save Viking Hotel, save everyone. Then you all cheer for me – "Hurrah for Sigurd! He brave! He clever! What we do without him?" So! I go fight this pig-dragon.'

And with that brave speech Sigurd strode across to the hotel, leaving the Ellises standing on the lawn, speechless. They huddled close together, clinging to each other with their arms.

'It's the end,' muttered Mr Ellis. 'We may as well close down now. Nobody will ever want to come back to the hotel after this.'

Inside The Viking Hotel, Sigurd crept up the stairs, holding Nosepicker at the ready. His eyes glinted fiercely in the darkness. It hadn't occurred to him to switch on the lights. 'Are you there, piggy-wig? I come to get you. I make you into bacon. Siggy find piggy. Here-coochy-coochy-coochy!'

Sigurd reached the first bedroom door. He paused a moment, took hold of the handle, counted to three and then burst in. 'Aha! Raaaargh!' His fierce battle cry was greeted with a startled scream as Mr and Mrs Ramsbottom leapt from their sleep. Mr Ramsbottom fell out of bed backwards and knocked himself out. Mrs Ramsbottom screamed that her husband was dead and fainted on the spot.

Sigurd searched under the bed. He opened the wardrobe and poked Nosepicker into every corner, filling the Ramsbottom's clothes with sword holes. There was no pig hiding there. He grunted and made for the next room.

'One, two, three – Aha! Raaaargh!'

Mr Travis was sitting up in bed watching television. He didn't even glance up at the Viking. 'Is that room service?' he said. 'It's about time you brought me that pot of tea. I've been waiting for . . . Good Heavens!' Mr Travis gave a muffled squeak as Sigurd lifted up one end of the bed and he found himself all rolled up in a bundle with the bed-covers.

The pig wasn't under the bed. Sigurd let it

crash back down and went off to continue his search next door. By this time Mrs Ramsbottom had come to her senses but, unfortunately, her husband had not. Still thinking he was dead, she pulled the poor man out of the bedroom by his feet and screamed for help.

Meantime Sigurd had reached the bathroom. He was about to throw open the door when it burst open itself, sending him crashing back against the wall. Out of the bathroom ran a pig that was almost as big as two tigers tied together, and three times as dangerous.

Her head was the size of a dustbin – a dustbin with fangs. Her body was as big as a car-crusher. She came out of the bathroom and stood on the landing. In her mouth were the remains of a lavatory brush. Somehow she had managed to get the shower-attachment wrapped round her head, a towel draped coyly over her enormous behind, and a toilet roll fixed to one rear trotter, where it now left a nice long trail of paper.

Another door opened further down the corridor, and a rather sleepy figure appeared. 'What's all the noise?' asked Mrs Tibblethwaite. 'What's going . . .' She froze with terror. The pig was glaring straight at her with hungry piggy-eyes. The sow opened and shut its jaws several times and took a couple of steps forward.

Mrs T. threw a frightened glance at her husband. 'Siggy?' she whispered. 'There is a very, very big pig looking at me and I'm scared. What do I do?' Before Sigurd could reply, the pig took three more menacing steps towards Mrs T. and pinned her against the wall, licking its chops noisily.

Sigurd gripped Nosepicker tightly and crept out from behind the bathroom door, inching towards the pig's fat rear. His face took on a fierce scowl and then, with a terrible war-cry, he leapt in the air. 'Ya-ha-raaaaargh!' He gave the sow's bulging behind an enormous prod with Nosepicker and the pig leapt into the air too, with a most peculiar, howling grunt.

'Snnnrrrghoowowowrrrgh!'

Again and again Sigurd poked the pig with his sword, driving the car-crusher down the stairs. As they passed the Ramsbottom's room Mrs Ramsbottom took one look at the pig and the roaring Viking and fainted again, right on top of her husband, making a nice neat heap.

A large roll of bedding staggered out from

bedroom number two and fell to the floor, where it spent a long time wriggling and squeaking before Mrs Tibblethwaite finally managed to get Mr Travis disentangled. Meanwhile Sigurd continued to drive the pig down the stairs, out into the garden and across to his newly-built pig-pen. He slammed the gate shut.

Everyone rushed to the fence and looked over at the new prisoner. 'Wow,' muttered Mr Ellis. 'That is some pig! You were brave Sigurd. I wouldn't have wanted to face an animal as big as that on my own.'

'Three cheers for Siggy!' cried Tim, and the Ellises all cheered, but it wasn't long before gloom and doom descended once again as several rather upset guests began to stumble outside.

Mr and Mrs Ellis calmed them down with cups of tea and quite a lot of brandy. Mrs Tibblethwaite got the Ramsbottoms safely back into bed. She seemed to have convinced Mrs Ramsbottom that it had all been a bad dream. 'I'll just have another sip of this,' twittered Mrs Ramsbottom, clutching Mrs T.'s silver hip-flask. 'It will help me sleep.'

Sigurd was even allowed to go back to his old room with his wife. 'Just for one night,' warned

Mr Ellis. 'We shall decide what to do in the morning.'

At last the Ellises themselves were able to go to bed. Zoe and Tim fell asleep the moment their heads touched the pillow but neither of their parents could sleep much. They were too busy worrying about what would happen the next day.

8   The Viking Village

The very first thing Mr Ellis did when he got up
the next morning was ring the local farm. He was
on the telephone for a long time. Mrs Ellis knew
that the farmer was a grumpy so-and-so, and
wouldn't take kindly to Sigurd 'borrowing' his
pigs. In fact she thought they would be lucky if
Sigurd didn't end up in court.

When her husband eventually managed to
get away from the telephone Mrs Ellis was
surprised to find him smiling. 'Mr Garret's
coming over this minute,' said Mr Ellis. 'You
won't believe this but he's delighted we've got the
pigs. Sigurd was telling the truth. The pigs broke
out from the farm yesterday evening. Garret's
been searching high and low all night. They're
worth several thousand pounds you know,
especially Big Betty.'

'Oh! Well that's a relief at any rate. The
Ramsbottoms don't seem to remember anything.
They're both complaining of headaches though –
I can't imagine why. Mr Travis has gone out to
the pen. He told me he wanted to see if that pig

was really as big as he thought it was last night.'

As soon as breakfast was over Tim and Zoe went out to see the pigs. Now that it was broad daylight they could see just how massive Big Betty was. She seemed quite happy, and none the worse for being poked with Nosepicker. Sigurd's wattle and daub fence looked pretty good too. Mr Travis was admiring the house that Sigurd had started.

'I've not seen a proper wattle and daub house actually being built, you know,' he mused. 'It's quite fascinating. Just like a proper Viking town. Sigurd ought to make a whole village.'

Zoe glanced at Tim, but he was busy scratching Big Betty's back with a long stick. She left her brother with Mr Travis and walked slowly back to the house in search of her parents.

'Mum? Dad? I've had an idea that might help things.' Zoe sounded so hesitant that both her parents looked at her with interest.

'Really?' said Mrs Ellis. 'What sort of idea?'

Zoe repeated what Mr Travis had said out by the pig-pen. 'It made me think,' she said. 'Maybe Sigurd could make a whole village – well, a small village, five or six houses maybe. He could even live out there. He could keep pigs and goats and chickens, like in a real Viking village.'

Mr Ellis laughed. 'It's a nice idea, Zoe. It would probably keep Siggy happy, but how would it help us?'

'Mr Travis said he thought it was fascinating. People would come to the hotel to see a Viking village with a real Viking.'

'Oh I don't think so,' said Mrs Ellis. 'People wouldn't come here just because there was a Viking village in the back garden.'

'Schools would,' said Zoe.

'Go on,' murmured Mr Ellis, rubbing his chin hard.

'Groups of school children could come here. They could learn about Flotby in Viking times and be part of a real Viking village, with a real Viking, and do real Viking things. Schools would think it was absolutely brilliant, and while they're in Flotby they would have to stay at our hotel.'

Mr Ellis hugged his daughter so hard she almost stopped breathing. 'That is a fantastic idea Zoe! It's totally amazing! Oh, it's so simple! Penny – what do you think?'

'I can't see how it can fail,' said Mrs Ellis. 'It's a stupendous idea, Zoe. Well done!'

'What's a stupendous idea?' asked a large, burly man with a tweed hat perched on top of his head.

'Ah, Mr Garret,' smiled Zoe's father. 'My daughter has just come up with a rather clever plan for our hotel. Let's see what you think of it. I'll tell you on the way out to Sigurd's pig-pen.'

They found Sigurd already out there, hard at work. He was inside the pen, building up the walls of his little house, while Mrs T. rubbed down one of the pigs. Mr Garret was highly surprised (and delighted) to see how well his pigs had been fenced in and looked after.

'You've got a natural way with farm animals,' he told Sigurd gruffly.

'I like pigs,' said Siggy. 'I like sheets and coats too, and wife.' He grinned at Mrs Tibblethwaite. 'Like wife most of all.'

'That's all right then,' smiled Mrs T., and gave him a kiss. 'You daft dumpling.'

'You must have been pretty good to get four pigs all the way down the road and shut up here,' said Mr Garret.

'We did have a bit of trouble with Big Betty,' said Mrs Ellis. 'But I'm glad you've got your pigs back.'

'How can I thank you?' Mr Garret asked. 'They're worth an awful lot to me.'

'There's no need for any thanks.'

But Mr Garret wanted to do something for the Ellises. He had been desperate when he had discovered the loss of his pigs, and he was genuinely delighted to have them back. 'Tell you what,' he said, 'this idea of young Zoe's – your Viking's going to need a few bits and pieces. He'll need hens for a start. I haven't got any sheep, but I have got an old billy goat he can keep here, and when Big Betty has her next litter he can come up to the farm and choose a piglet.'

Sigurd listened to this with growing excitement. He rushed across to Mr Garret, wrapped the poor farmer in his arms, kissed him on both cheeks and then rubbed noses with him.

'Gerroff!' shouted Mr Garret, trying to push Sigurd away. 'You big hairy ox!'

'You good man!' cried the Viking. 'I pray to Thor and tell him you very good and go to Valhalla when you die.' Sigurd turned to Mr Ellis. 'You good man too!' he roared, and opened his arms wide. 'Come to Siggy!'

'Oh no,' muttered Mr Ellis, backing away. 'No Siggy, leave me alone. I don't want to be hugged. Siggy! Go away!' He turned tail and fled, with Sigurd in hot pursuit. The others watched with delight.

'I never knew Dad could run that fast,' said Tim. A startled scream came from the far side of the hotel. Mrs Ellis giggled.

'He can't,' she said.

The KoW is now!-
well, almost.

QUESTION:

What do you get if you cross a modern-day superhero and eco warrior with abseiling cows, fake blood and Jamie, a boy who is desperate to become the most famous film director ever?

ANSWER:

Krazy Kow Saves the World – Well, Almost.
The chaotic and *udderly* fantastic new novel by Jeremy Strong and illustrated by Nick Sharratt.

Katch the Kow
1 August 2002

Jeremy talks!

Born: Eltham, south-east London,
18 November 1949

Lives: Kent

First book: *Smith's Tail*, 1978

When did you start writing? When I was about six, but I was about eight when I began to feel that writing stories – inventing things and using my imagination – was absolutely brilliant.

Where do you get your ideas? Anywhere and everywhere – from my head, from places, things I see or hear, from history, from friends ... The best ideas usually come when I'm not thinking about writing at all.

When you start writing a new story do you have a set routine?
I hate starting, but once I am sitting at the computer I usually get on a roll. Once the first version is complete I read aloud to myself and our two cats, so I can hear the characters and feel how the story flows.

Do you mind being interrupted when you are writing?
The worst culprit for interrupting me is our youngest cat Moses. He sits by the monitor and tries to catch the cursor. But most of all he likes writing himself. He stands with both front paws on my keyboard and then all I get is mmmmmmmmw-------88888888888888;;;;;;;;;;;;;kkkkkkkkkkkkk.........

What is the best part about writing funny stories?
I love making other people laugh and seeing smiles on their faces. I like it when I'm writing and I suddenly think of a really funny bit and it makes me laugh too. I wanted to be a writer ever since I was a child, and here I am doing just that, so I think I am a very lucky person. (I also wanted to be a Grand Prix racing driver.)

And finally, what is your all-time favourite thing to eat?
For everyday noshing I would choose fried egg, bacon, chips and mushrooms and for dessert I would have chocolate roulade. (Also, I ADORE cheese!)

Jeremy Strong

To find out more about Jeremy Strong, click on to:
www.jeremystrong.co.uk or www.puffin.co.uk

14 ½ THINGS YOU DIDN'T KNOW ABOUT JEREMY STRONG...

1. Jeremy used to kiss his teddy bear 'good-night' every single night.

2. Jeremy once fell backwards off a swing and cracked his head open. It needed stitches.

3. He used to play electric violin in a rock band called THE INEDIBLE CHEESE SANDWICH.

4. Jeremy likes to relax by getting into a deep, hot bath with lots of bubbles and candles round the edge.

5. When he was five he sat on a heater and burnt his ***.

6. Jeremy used to look after a dog that kept eating his underpants. (No – NOT while he was wearing them!)

7. He is hopeless at Maths – and lots of other things.

8. He gave up learning the piano when he was nine, and he wishes he hadn't.

9. He used to bite his nails and didn't stop until he was twenty-seven.

10. His grandmother used to ride a huge Harley Davidson motorbike – in the 1920s!

11. His nickname at primary school was 'Pongo'! (He didn't like it very much!)

12. Jeremy doesn't like puddings very much, especially hot, steamy ones.

13. He's scared of beasties that go 'buzz buzz'.

14. Jeremy's starting to go bald!

and a half ... He's got big feet.

Jeremy loves to write about crazy characters and potty places. See if you can find them in the 'silly search' below.
(There are 12 to spot)

Z	Y	G	H	I	I	W	A	G	T	C
P	C	R	U	N	C	H	B	A	G	A
Q	U	E	Q	O	J	K	X	A	S	P
W	L	E	P	M	V	C	U	I	D	T
I	G	N	O	O	J	D	Z	K	U	A
T	N	J	X	T	Y	P	F	H	K	I
T	I	E	L	O	Y	C	N	K	E	N
S	N	L	M	I	G	E	Q	R	O	B
E	T	L	Q	N	R	Y	E	O	F	L
N	H	Y	I	S	G	K	H	V	D	A
D	G	K	H	U	A	Z	Q	L	O	C
V	I	O	L	E	T	Q	X	A	R	K
V	L	C	R	A	G	B	N	T	K	P
B	M	T	K	O	P	T	W	E	I	A
U	S	O	T	W	Q	Z	I	P	L	T
L	Z	J	E	R	E	M	Y	Q	T	C
D	I	N	O	S	A	U	R	B	D	H

1. **Streaker** – from *The Hundred-Mile-an-Hour Dog* ✓
2. **Petal Vork** – from *I'm Telling You, They're Aliens!*
3. **Lightning Lucy** – from *Lightning Lucy*
4. **Crunchbag** – from *My Dad's Got an Alligator*
5. **Witts End** – the primary school from *Pirate Pandemonium*
6. **Captain Blackpatch** – from *The Indoor Pirates on Treasure Island*
7. **(Mrs) Green-Jelly** – from *My Granny's Great Escape*
8. **Violet** – from *Pandemonium at School*
9. **Duke of Dork** – from *The Karate Princess in Monsta Trouble*
10. **Dinosaur**
11. **Viking** – from *Viking at School*
12. **Jeremy**

Laugh? I couldn't stop!

How many crazy Jeremy Strong books have you read?

The Desperate Adventures
of Sir Rupert and Rosie Gusset

Sir Rupert and Rosie Gusset
in Deadly Danger

Dinosaur Pox
The Hundred-Mile-an-Hour Dog
I'm Telling You, They're Aliens!
The Indoor Pirates
The Indoor Pirates on Treasure Island
The Karate Princess
The Karate Princess in Monsta Trouble
The Karate Princess
and the Cut-throat Robbers

Lightning Lucy
My Granny's Great Escape
Pirate Pandemonium
There's a Viking in my Bed
and Other Stories

Check out more titles by Jeremy @
www.puffin.co.uk or www.jeremystrong.co.uk

Choosing a brilliant book
can be a tricky business...
but not any more

www.puffin.co.uk

The best selection of books at your fingertips

So get clicking!

Searching the site is easy – you'll find
what you're looking for at the click of a mouse,
from great authors to brilliant books and more!